What do you think of your new bed, Simon?
You like it?

BARK! BARK!

Okay, Simon. Let's go for a walk.
You can try out your new bed
when we get back!

Simon's New Bed

by Christian Trimmer · art by Melissa van der Paardt

A atheneum

Atheneum Books for Young Readers
New York London Toronto Sydney New Delhi

Simon couldn't remember the last time he was so excited. This was going to be the best nap of his life.

He quickly rehydrated.

And then he sprinted to the room he shared with
his best friend, the boy . . .

only to discover a problem.

Excuse me, Miss Adora Belle.
You're in the wrong bed. That's my new bed.

Since politeness didn't work, Simon tried other methods to get Miss Adora Belle off his bed.

He howled.

He barked.

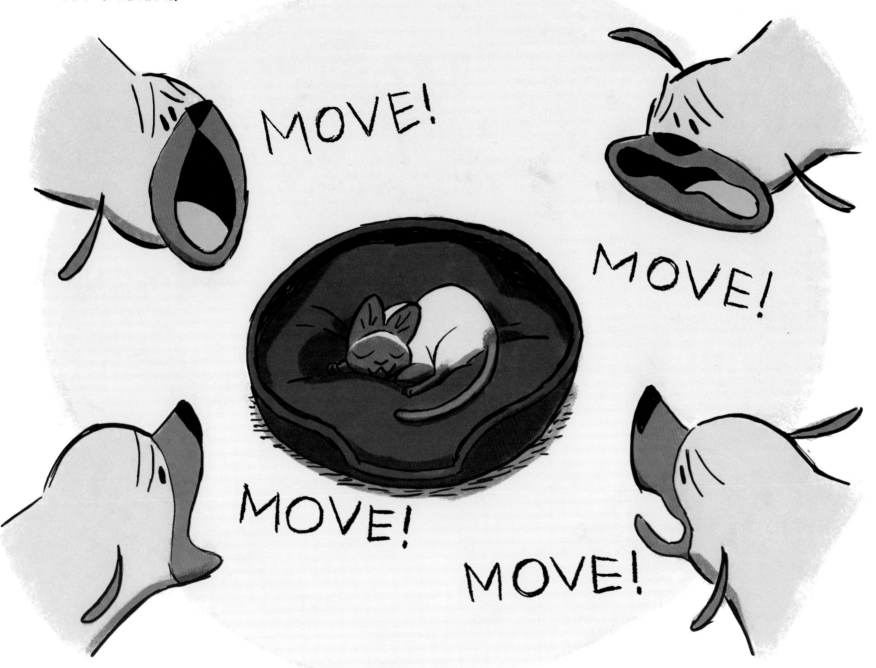

He dragged her from his room, down the hall, into the kitchen, under the dining room table, out the back door, through the yard, up the front steps, and back to his room.

But like all cats, Miss Adora Belle had a you've-got-to-see-it-to-believe-it sense of balance.

Then Simon tried giving her
a taste of her own medicine.

LET'S SEE HOW SHE
LIKES IT.

Miss Adora Belle didn't seem to mind.

He even tried to trick her.

Still nothing.
Simon realized he had only one option left—
one shameful, embarrassing option.

He begged.

Pleeeeeeeeease.
Get out.
Of.
My.
BED!!!

But Miss Adora Belle didn't.

Move.
An.
Inch.

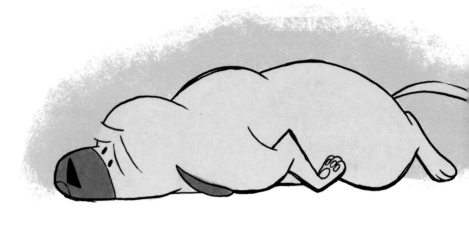

Simon was on the verge of tears.
He had tried everything he could think of
to get that mean ol' cat off his new bed.

But what if . . .

Miss Adora Belle, how about we . . .

...share?

Simon didn't relish the idea of sharing
his bed with Miss Adora Belle
for his very first nap on it.

But sometimes . . .

you have to pick your battles.

For Britton,
a thoughtful and generous brother and friend —C. T.

For my family and friends,
who mean the world to me —M. V. D. P.

atheneum

ATHENEUM BOOKS FOR YOUNG READERS
An imprint of Simon & Schuster Children's Publishing Division
1230 Avenue of the Americas, New York, New York 10020
Text copyright © 2015 by Christian Trimmer
Illustrations and hand-lettering copyright © 2015 by Melissa van der Paardt
For information about special discounts for bulk purchases, please contact Simon & Schuster Special Sales
at 1-866-506-1949 or business@simonandschuster.com.
The Simon & Schuster Speakers Bureau can bring authors to your live event.
For more information or to book an event, contact the Simon & Schuster Speakers Bureau
at 1-866-248-3049 or visit our website at www.simonspeakers.com.
Book design by Lauren Rille
The text for this book is set in A Font With Serifs.
The illustrations for this book are digitally rendered.
Manufactured in the United States of America
0915 PCR
10 9 8 7 6 5 4 3 2
Library of Congress Cataloging-in-Publication Data
Trimmer, Christian.
Simon's new bed / Christian Trimmer ; illustrated by Melissa van der Paardt. — First edition.
pages cm
Summary: "A humorous picture book about a dog's new bed being taken over by a cat"— Provided by publisher.
ISBN 978-1-4814-3019-7 (hardcover : alk. paper)
ISBN 978-1-4814-3020-3 (eBook)
[1. Dogs—Fiction. 2. Cats—Fiction. 3. Humorous stories.] I. Van der Paardt, Melissa, illustrator. II. Title.
PZ7.1.J56Si 2015
[E]—dc23   2014023581